WATERSHIP™ DOWN

Hazel Raids the Farm

Diane Redmond

RED FOX

A Red Fox Book

Published by Random House Children's Books
20 Vauxhall Bridge Road, London SW1V 2SA

A division of The Random House Group Ltd
London Melbourne Sydney Auckland
Johannesburg and agencies throughout the world

www.watershipdown.net

Illustrations by County Studio, Leicester

1 3 5 7 9 10 8 6 4 2

Printed and bound in Italy

THE RANDOM HOUSE GROUP Limited Reg. No. 954009

www.randomhouse.co.uk

ISBN 0 09 940808 2

**This story represents scenes from the television series, Watership Down,
which is inspired by Richard Adams' novel of the same name.**

Hannah was blowing dandelion seeds into the air, when Hazel came out of the warren.

'You're up early,' the mouse said. 'Is anything wrong?'

Hazel stared across the valley. 'I'm worried about the future,' he said. 'The warren needs more rabbits.'

Hannah skipped excitedly. 'There are some rabbits at Nuthanger Farm,' she said. 'They live in a cage.'

Hazel smiled. 'Then I'm going to rescue them!'

Hazel went into the warren and woke his brother.

Fiver opened one eye. 'I was having a nice dream,' he grumbled.

'Get up,' urged Hazel. 'We've got work to do.'

Outside, they bumped into little Pipkin.

'Do you want to go on an adventure?' asked Hazel.

'Oh yes!' squeaked Pipkin.

The rabbits were halfway down the hill when Kehaar flew up to them. 'Where you go?' he screeched.

'To the farm,' said Hazel. 'We're going to rescue the hutch-rabbits.'

'Be careful of fat cat and noisy dog,' warned the gull.

At the farm, the rabbits hid behind some milk churns.

'Hannah said the rabbits are in there,' said Hazel, pointing to the barn. 'Now follow me.'

'What about the dog?' asked Pipkin, nervously.

'Don't worry,' said Hazel. 'He's asleep.'

Cautiously, the rabbits crossed the yard.

At the barn, Hazel looked around. There was no sign of any danger. 'Fiver, come with me,' he said. 'Pipkin, you stay here and keep watch.'

None of them saw Tabitha, the farm cat, slip behind the milk churns. Her green eyes glinted and her tail twitched as she watched Hazel and Fiver go into the barn.

Hazel hopped up onto the hay bales and peeped into the rabbit hutch. 'Hello in there,' he said.

A doe called Clover put her nose to the wire mesh. 'Where's your cage? she asked.

'I don't have a cage. I live outside,' said Hazel.

'Who feeds you?' asked Boxwood, a large buck.

'I feed myself,' said Hazel.

Down below Fiver was getting impatient. 'Quickly, Hazel,' he said. 'I smell danger!'

Hazel started chewing the leather hinges on the top of the cage. 'We've come to help you escape,' he told the farm rabbits. 'When the door opens, get ready to run!'

Fiver hopped outside. 'Everything all right, Pipkin?' he asked.

Pipkin nodded. 'No sign of the cat.' But at that moment Tabitha came flying towards them, with her claws outstretched.

Fiver pulled Pipkin into the barn. They scampered across to the hay bales. 'Hazel, hurry,' he cried. 'The cat's after us!'

When the farm rabbits saw the cat they scrambled back into their cage. Only Clover stayed with Hazel.

'Fiver, take Clover and Pipkin with you,' said Hazel. 'I'll fight off the cat.'

As the rabbits ran towards the barn door, Tabitha sprang again, but this time Hazel blocked her path. 'Get back, you stinking cat!' he cried.

Pipkin, Fiver and Clover fled across the farmyard. Chester
the dog was still sleeping, but when he smelt the rabbits
he leapt to his feet and started barking.

Inside the barn, Tabitha was creeping towards Hazel.
'Give up, long-ears,' she hissed.

'No!' cried Hazel and with a leap he jumped over the cat's head and raced out of the barn.

'Woof! Woof! Woof!' barked Chester, as Hazel sped past.

Hearing the noise, the farmer came out of the house, carrying a rifle. When he saw the rabbit, he carefully took aim and Boom! Hazel collapsed on the ground.

In the bushes nearby, Fiver, Pipkin and Clover trembled.

'What was that?' gasped Pipkin.

'A fire-stick,' said Clover. 'Man uses it to kill from far away.'

Pipkin's ears drooped. 'Has he… has he got Hazel?'

'I don't know,' said Fiver. 'But if you take Clover back to Watership Down, I'm going to look.'

Hazel had injured his back leg. In pain, he limped along the side of the lane and collapsed in a ditch. Hearing the heavy crunch of the farmer's boots coming closer, he pulled himself into a drainage pipe to hide. When the farmer looked in the ditch he saw nothing, and walked on.

Back on Watership Down, Bigwig,
Blackberry and Hawkbit were getting
ready for the arrival of the new rabbits.

'What time did Hazel say he'd be back?'
Bigwig asked Kehaar.

'Before sun go away,' said the gull.

'He's late,' said Bigwig, anxiously.
'Will you go and look for them?'

'OK!' cried Kehaar, and with a loud
screech he set off for Nuthanger Farm.

Fiver was searching the lane when the gull arrived. 'Oh, Kehaar,' he gasped. 'Hazel's been hit by a fire-stick…'

'Then we must find him quick!' screeched the gull. 'You got special way of seeing. Look!'

Fiver closed his eyes and concentrated hard. Then he heard a faint voice, like a whisper: *Fiver… find me…*

'Hazel's alive!' he cried. 'It sounded like he was inside something.'

'OK,' said the gull. 'So we look in all inside places!'

Kehaar poked his long beak into hollow logs and Fiver looked under hedges. When he came to the pipe, his ears started to twitch. 'Hazel's in there!' he shouted. 'I know it!'

They scrambled into the pipe and found Hazel lying on his side.

'Fiver... I knew you'd come,' he said.

'I heard you calling,' said Fiver.

'But I didn't,' said Hazel, confused.

'Then your spirit did. It told me where to find you,' Fiver whispered.

Kehaar began stabbing his beak into the bleeding wound.

'Ow!' cried Hazel. 'That hurts!'

The gull pecked out the pellet and Fiver licked the wound clean, then Hazel fell asleep.

'He better after sleep,' said Kehaar.

Later, Kehaar and Fiver helped Hazel back to Watership Down. At the top of the hill, all the rabbits rushed out to meet them.

Clover hopped up to Hazel. 'I never thought I'd see outside,' she said. 'Thank you for rescuing me.'

'I'm glad you're here,' said Hazel. 'I'm only sorry the others didn't make it, too.'

'Don't be,' said Clover. 'They like that cage. They're happy where they are.'

With a thud Kehaar landed beside Hazel. 'Must rest,' he said. 'Best thing for you.'

'Come with me, Hazel,' said Hannah. 'I've made you a nice fresh bed.'

Hazel hopped towards the warren, but before going inside he stopped to watch the sun set, a sad look in his eyes.

'What are you thinking?' asked Fiver.

'About another place,' said Hazel. 'I promised Primrose I'd go back for her. It will be dangerous, but we must return to Efrafa.'